"Beautiful prose, poi̲ theme of hope out of asnes, will enchant readers as this tender Christmas story unfolds with the whimsy of a fairy tale and the heart of a giant. Truly, Amanda Dykes is an exquisite wordsmith and consummate storyteller, captivating my every thought as Giovanni, Aria, and James tentatively reach for the broken pieces of their lives that seem impossibly and forever fragmented. The spiritual themes are captivating and stirring - be prepared to be inspired and moved...

... If you only read one Christmas story this year, ensure it is *Bespoke*."

—REL MOLLET, editor/reviewer,
RelzReviewz.com, Novel Crossing contributor,
Family Fiction correspondent

"A joyful gem of a story, pulsing with warmth and light, *Bespoke* has all the ingredients of a first class read – characters of substance, a hint of mystery, heartfelt romance, and gorgeous prose. Encore, Amanda Dykes!"

—LAURA FRANTZ, award-winning author
of *Love's Reckoning*

"Cozy, sweet and whimsical, *Bespoke* is everything one would wish for a Christmas story to be. Yet author Amanda Dykes masterfully layers in a quiet and thought-provoking depth that takes the reader by the heart and doesn't let go, even after the last page is turned."

—JOANNE BISCHOF, award-winning author
of *This Quiet Sky*

"A little story with a big heart, Bespoke captured me with its polished, intelligent prose and characters both winsome and layered, and held me in its spell with a poignant yearning-to uncover the painful secrets of the characters' past and see the unfolding of a future shining with the promise of joy. Amanda Dykes is a fresh and compelling voice in fiction and *Bespoke: A Tiny Christmas Tale* sings with a timeless song of rebirth."

—LORI BENTON, award-winning author of
Burning Sky and *The Pursuit of Tamsen Littlejohn*

"A gloriously music-infused fable forged by grace. The experience in its carefully plotted and lyrical pages is not unlike a cup of apple cider as embers dance and shadows fall. I mean to make it an annual seasonal read. I think of this story and my heart-strings tug a little while a smile curves. It is not just a story, it is now a dear friend.

Marrying the eerie beauty of classical composition with a quaint little town --just pitch-perfect ---and filled with snow, holly and hope, Dykes proves her craft with every poetical line. Part love story, with fable-like essence and all faith and charity, *Bespoke* is that rare, cherished glimmery find…Radiant."

—RACHEL MCMILLAN, author of *A Singular and Whimsical Problem.* Writer/reviewer, Breakpoint, Novel Crossing, A Fair Substitute for Heaven

Bespoke

A TINY CHRISTMAS TALE

AMANDA DYKES

Lanternwood Press

Bespoke: a Tiny Christmas Tale

© 2014, 2015 Amanda Dykes

For permission requests or other inquiries, contact the author at

www.AmandaDykes.com

Scriptures quoted from The Holy Bible, King James Version, public domain.

Printed in the United States of America

Lanternwood Press
Zephyr Cove, Nevada
Library of Congress Control Number: 2015913288
Paperback ISBN: 978-0-692-49191-1
E-book ISBN: 978-1-311-53070-7

Author is represented by Wendy Lawton of Books and Such Literary Management.

Cover design by Amanda Dykes

"The LORD is my strength and song,
and is become my salvation."
Psalm 118:14, KJV

To the girl whose words dance with light
&
The boy whose laughter is alive with music.

May you always have a song.

- PROLOGUE -

WHISPERS ABOUT THE SECRET Symphony of Giovanni St. John filled the world from every direction: The symphony that tempted fate. The symphony with a name shrouded in mystery. The one no one would ever, ever hear... or so Giovanni St. John said.

It was his ninth symphony, and as superstition had it, a composer must never write beyond his ninth symphony. To do so was to face certain death.

But thunder lived inside Giovanni St. John, and speculations over his ninth symphony flew by the time he'd penned his fifth. Even the queen placed a wager. Giovanni St. John was an unstoppable force, she said, who would pay no heed to a silly superstition. Yes, he had his quirks—his refusal to conduct unless he used his own baton, for example. Still, a great like St. John was allowed a few peculiarities. Peculiarities were not the same as superstition.

With each year, his force grew stronger. The Palais Andelle tore down a three-hundred-year-old wall to make room for a bigger audience, all to win the honor of hosting the premier of his sixth.

For his seventh symphony, he conducted with such fervor that when he raised his hand in the final movement for the famous four-measure rest, it trembled. In the silence, he slowly, slowly turned all three-hundred-and-sixty degrees to take in the faces of the audience. They held their breath. His power was palpable. When he resumed, the relief in the room flowed like a tide, surging with the swells and pulls of the finale. It was as if he'd written their collective exhale straight into the sheet music.

His eighth symphony set the world afire with rumors of his imminent demise. Surely his next would be his last. Why, Ludwig Van Beethoven himself never made it beyond his ninth. Schubert, too, and Dvořák. The queen countered again that the brooding man who dominated the stage of the world would never ascribe to such fables. He held fate in his iron-fisted grip.

But neither side knew Giovanni St. John as they supposed. For on the closing night of his eighth symphony, at the end of the London season, he laid down his legendary baton and vanished clean away for nine solid years. No one knew where. No one knew why.

Then, just when they all counted him lost, he re-emerged, brow furrowed deeper than ever, music alive with a new fury.

He'd written his tenth.

The ninth is there, he'd said. *But you'll never know it. Never hear it. Never see it. Here is my tenth. I'm alive. Listen.*

Listen, they did, for fifteen years and six symphonies more, each more tightly coiled with crescendos than the last. Yet every performance was cloaked with the intrigue of the Secret Symphony. Crowds flocked more than ever to his concerts, but when he made his trademark three-hundred-and-sixty-degree turn, he saw not captivation but speculation. When he lifted his baton he felt their hunger, not for his current masterpiece, but for the one he would not share. And oh, did that ignite his wrath.

Legends continued to pass through opera halls from ear to listening ear. Some said he kept the hidden music in a safe in an Alpen castle dungeon. One tale claimed the missing symphony was encapsulated in the cornerstone of an Italian abbey. Others said it travelled with him always—to every soul-quaking performance, in every country. The only thing *he* ever said was that he'd take the secret to his grave.

But the day Giovanni St. John took to his death bed, his secret symphony began to live.

- CHAPTER I -

THE TOWNSPEOPLE OF THE ISLAND called it the Silent House.

James Shaw wished more than anything he could forget it—forget the way it loomed over the village, the thatched roof that sagged where it used to shine, the dark stone walls and the empty rooms that echoed with memories of music cut short.

Most of all, he longed to forget the oppressive truth: the silence was his own fault.

But the Silent House would not forget him. There it stood, day and night, casting a shadow over his humble blacksmith's forge. He tried not to look at it, tried not to remember the fair face and long, dark curls of the girl who used to cross her eyes and puff her cheeks out at him through the gable window when they were children. That window, just there, three stories up and two windows to the right. Where once upon a time, she'd light a candle for him on nights when the moon was bright and the sky clear, its message their secret: *Meet me at the dune tonight.* He'd bring the bucket, she'd bring a net, and they'd gather whichever sea-washed treasures shimmered under the night sky.

There were days when he could almost make it through without remembering, but something—a sound in the street, a game on the Castlebury green, or just a memory on the wind—would pull his concentration from his mallet and anvil. And then the sparks from his forge would still and the shadow would entangle him once more.

On this icy afternoon, it was a loud, out-of-place clatter that disrupted his focus.

In the summer months, when the sun-stretched

days were long and warm, visitors filled the cobbled streets of the tiny Isle of Espoir. Some came from France, some from England, for Espoir lay halfway in between. But in the winter months, when the wet chill descended and his forge was the warmest place in the entire Isle, there were never visitors.

Never. Except today. When a team of matched bays and a grand carriage with deep red curtains draping its windows rattled down the street. James hadn't seen such a sight for fifteen years.

He set down his mallet, moved past the mound of dancing orange coals, and leaned his hand against the stone-arched doorway as the carriage halted in front of the Silent House.

The carriage door opened on the opposite side, away from his view. The angle prevented him from seeing anything but two slippered feet as they touched down on the street, and the hem of a dress, blue like the ocean at dusk.

A woman, then. And a brave one, to face the spitting skies on this cold November day.

He heard a murmur as she spoke to someone inside the carriage, and then he saw the back of her dark twisting braid and a set of slim shoulders as she traverses the steps up to the front gate. She ran a hand up the slanted stone wall as she went, skipping the mortared seams as if she knew them by heart.

With every step she took, his certainty grew: this was her. Aria.

She paused at the gate, one hand on the treble clef scroll he'd wrought with his own tools. Then she turned, and for a single beat, the years and stories dividing them dropped away. Those dark eyes, sadder even than the last time he'd seen them, rested on him with a flicker of something that made him ache. She clutched a scroll of paper tied with a thick red ribbon in her other hand. With an odd and urgent movement, she pulled her cape over it and stared down at the ground.

The carriage jostled, and another form joined her. Familiar. Radiating the commanding presence the man had always possessed, even if he was hunched over slightly and the hand he used to beckon Aria trembled just a bit.

Aria leaned in to listen. James knew he shouldn't be watching, but he couldn't take his eyes off of the pair of them: this father and daughter, who'd sworn never to return.

Aria nodded and with one last lightning-quick glance at James, she turned and took the remaining steps up to the door. He watched as the Silent House swallowed her into its still, dark halls.

So. Here they were again. James Shaw and Giovanni St. John, alone with only a cobbled street and stretch of green between them... the very grass where the man had once stood, shaking with fury, giving James a warning he'd never forget.

Perhaps the man wouldn't see him. Or perhaps he wouldn't recognize him. Perhaps...

Their eyes met. He took one step toward James, stopped, and shook his head one slow, solitary time before climbing the steps into his house. Formidable. Unforgiving. And rightly so.

That night, despite his best efforts to avoid it, James found himself standing before the window over his workbench. His eyes traveled their old familiar path: Across the cobblestones, up three stories, and two windows to the right. And there, in her gable, a single flame flickered.

- CHAPTER 2 -

IT WAS LIKE ANY OTHER sitting room, really, except for the rows upon rows of brass instruments lining the walls. Aria stepped in, running her hands lightly over the French horn mounted nearest the reaching oak door. The instrument's weaving curves caught the firelight, bouncing the reflection on to a trumpet, which passed the gleam along to a trombone. On it went, floor to ceiling and all around, this dance of light and brass.

Once upon a time it had been her, flitting from instrument to instrument as the light did now. She recalled the cold weight of each, the thrill of a song yet unplayed. So foreign, now.

"You're as silent as the night, Aria."

There they were again, those words Father loved to speak. But this time, instead of embarrassing her, they quickened her pulse with thoughts of her plan. Did he know? He couldn't. He mustn't.

His voice was gravelly. A weariness in every word tugged on her heart. The end of his days was near, and she had much to do still. So much to show him...

The logs in the fireplace crackled, and she took a seat next to the hearth. Setting her papers aside she retrieved a poker with her stronger hand to stir the embers. Warmth and light... and the power to destroy. Or transform, she reminded herself as she stared into the flames. She was counting on it.

"What are you working on?" Father gestured an arm to point at her small pile of papers beside her. "More of your...equations?" Even with fatigue weighing down his words, she could still hear a touch of pride in his voice. He'd always told her numbers were the backbone to any proper symphony. He watched her, light flickering over his weathered face, his silver-flecked chestnut hair.

"Yes," she said, biting her lip to keep from chattering on as she yearned to. Just more of her numbers and lines. But this time, if her idea worked, the numbers would mend a rift decades-old.

She cleared her throat, eager to change the subject. "Are you comfortable, father?" She had work to do, but couldn't bring herself to leave him alone if he was hurting. For a man who'd travelled the world ten times over and held the rapt attention of thousands upon thousands of people, he was as alone as could possibly be. For all his fame—or perhaps because of it—he had only her.

"Mmm," he said, waving her question away. "I'm fine. Just considering the best formation for the strings section."

"For Christmas Eve?" She pulled two blankets from the fireside basket: one to tuck around Father, one to cover what she was about to take.

"It must be unlike any other performance," he said, and the quiet resolve in his voice told her again what she already knew: it would be his last.

"Have you decided which symphony?" The island orchestra, if one could even call them that, was a bare-bones crew of farmers, fishermen, and shopkeepers who proudly played two times a year on the highest dune on the island. "Treble Clef upon Trouble Cliff," they called themselves, always with a hearty laugh. For Father to even consider conducting at such a venue, with such an orchestra... something had changed in him.

He closed his eyes and the corner of his mouth tugged upward into an almost-smile. "The Seventh," he said. "I think we'll play the Seventh."

Of course. The only one that had captivated his audience as much as his un-played ninth.

"The final movement," he opened one eye to look at her for a moment, then shut it again. "Their bones will be frozen clean through if we try for more."

"Good." She bent to take his hand. "That was

always my favorite." Something about that four-measure rest, as if it were waiting on life itself.

"You'll..." he closed his eyes. "You'll come?"

Aria stilled, letting the two words sink in. Never, ever had she been allowed anywhere near one of his symphonies. Except, of course, the ninth... but they had all worked very hard to forget that. Father said the people were too nosey, that they'd only gawk at her and he would never allow that—so she'd spent her years at boarding school, known only as simple Aria Johnson.

"I'll come, Father." She could barely form the words, so shocked was she. His breathing steadied into deep draws of sleep. Even in slumber, intensity lived there. She stood, carefully spread the first blanket over his lap, then moved about the room gathering the things she'd need. She tucked an awkward bundle beneath the blanket draped over her arm and slipped out of the room. This wouldn't be the first time she'd smuggled something dear to her father out of his house and over to the blacksmith's. This time, though, it wouldn't end in disaster.

The hallway was dark, but she knew every square inch of the grand village house. Following her old familiar path to the servant's stairs, she tiptoed past the kitchen where Barnes sat scratching his pen across plain stationary. Barnes was the only servant Father trusted enough to bring back to the island, and the man spent every evening the same way: penning letters. To whom, Aria did not know.

Before she could change her mind, Aria stepped into a night so cold it pierced her lungs. Moonlight glanced across the sheen of her blue skirt and on across the village green, marking her path.

Just meters from the forge she paused, watching James through the window. He was grown, now, but the same dark hair and somber eyes intense as blue flame. He stood over the forge just as he used to and she watched him pound, pound, pound a rod of iron, twist it, pound, pound, pound again, twist it. Expert beats, the perfect quarter-time tempo of a master smith. But with each turn, the lines of his chiseled face grew grimmer.

She was transfixed, listening to him send his music into the night. To the cadence of his work she stepped closer and closer, tilting her head to make sense of what she saw.

He'd once been in charge of the foundry—the other half of the shop where metals were melted, refined, cast into sand molds and cooled into their new form. It suited him, he'd always said, giving things new shape. Yet here he was now, on the forge side instead, where his older brothers had once reigned with their heating and pounding.

Three signs above the door attested to this change, too. One below the other, swinging in the breeze.

Shaw and Sons

Bespoke Metalwork

Forge

...Not "Forge and Foundry," as it had said when she was a girl.

A slamming door at the back of the building snapped her to attention. James was gone from his window.

She clutched her bundle beneath her cape and willed herself up to the weathered wooden door. She lifted a hand, stiffer than usual, to knock.

When her knock went unanswered and all was quiet inside, she lifted the latch and let herself in. This was a place of business, after all. And on the island, business hours were whenever someone needed something. Even so, she knew she shouldn't be here. If Father knew...

Warmth from the fires inside enveloped her and she took a step into the room, so familiar with the scent of coal smoke mingled with the sweetness of hot metal. Nobody in sight. The old stump James had brought inside for her chair during their games of marbles all those years ago still stood right in its old spot, next to the overturned pail he'd perched on in his gangly youth.

Something dark and small, just the size of one of their polished pebbles, rested on her stump.

Was that--? No, surely... surely he wouldn't have kept it. She picked it up, turned it in her hand. The rock's smooth surface was mapped in her mind from years gone by. Carefully, she set it back down and scanned the rest of the room.

The canvas-draped casting table stood like a solitary ghost in the corner to her right, far from the reach of stray sparks. She set her bundle down atop it, lifted a corner of the rough cloth—

"Please don't," a low voice said behind her. Steadiness and depth in that voice—and an edge of something broken.

Aria turned, and there he was. James. The one she'd have run to with a string of laughter trailing behind her once. ...But now he stood, every inch a man. A stranger, almost, though his brown hair fell tousled over his forehead just as it always had after a long day's work. White shirtsleeves pushed up to his elbows, arms full of firewood, his stance was marked with a gravity bigger than the room could hold.

"James," she said. "I mean—Mr. Shaw..."

His dark brows pushed together and he drew back ever-so-slightly. "Miss St. John." His tone was cold. He moved across the room, began unloading the wood into a perfectly patterned stack against the wall. "We're closed."

We? Aria scanned the perimeter of the room again. One tin cup hanging on the wall. One Blacksmith's apron pushed by a breeze on its nail by the door. By all counts "Shaw and Sons" was now just one man: the youngest son.

"I'm sorry," she said. "I'll go." She made for the door, but her glove snagged on an ash pail perched on a shelf. It clanged to the ground, a cloud engulfing her. With a cough she scrambled to scoop up her mess.

"Let me." He knelt and placed one hand against her arm to still her, voice low. Even through the satin of the glove, even past the barrier of numbness that lived always in her arms, she could feel his warmth and strength.

"Aria," he said, shaking his head. A thrill shot through her, to hear him speak her name. He sat back on his heels, settling his gaze on her in his old steadiness at last. "What are you doing here?" The words would have sounded cold, were it not for the trace of wonder threading them together.

"I'm—just—"

"It's been fifteen years."

"I know." She hung her head. "I should have written you." And might he... have tried to write her? The fear that he hadn't stung, though she knew very well that her father had ensured no letters from James Shaw could ever reach her. "I should have at least sent word."

James shook his head. "I never expected you to write. Not after..." he cleared his throat. "I just didn't think you'd ever come back here."

What could she say to that? That being ripped away from her best friend, from this island, had unraveled her? That she'd wanted to return a thousand times? She leaned back into scooping the dust but he stilled her once more, letting his hand linger this time. He, one of three people in all the world, knew what the gloves covered. *It's not your fault, James*. The words beat against her ribs, trying to find a way out.

He cleared his throat and put his full concentration into scooping up the ashes. "You still have that habit, you know."

"Which habit?" She continued smoothing the fine white dust into a pile on the floor, despite the look he gave her.

"Ignoring the questions you don't want to answer." He cocked a dark brow, a smile dawning. The first she'd seen on him as a grown man. "What are you doing here?"

She darted a glance at her parcel on the casting table. "I'm here to try and undo the mess I've made," she said. By the way he narrowed his eyes, it would seem he knew she wasn't just talking about ashes.

He followed the direction of her gaze. "In what

way?"

She pursed her lips. This was going to sound peculiar, no matter how she put it. But it was now or never. "I need your help."

He stood, hand outstretched to help her. Such a simple gesture, and yet in it she felt more at home than all the hours she'd spent in the Silent House since arriving. Setting the pail aside, he moved to unfold the woolen grey blanket.

"Wait. First... let me show you this." She pulled out the scroll from inside her cape pocket and handed it to him. Curiosity marked his face as he slid the red string off, paper crinkling as he unrolled it.

She watched the familiar dark lashes narrow around those blue eyes. Concentration.   Analysis. Quick understanding of what he saw before him and then—a shadow. "You want to make this?"

Aria nodded. "Together," she said, gesturing a circle in the space between them.

"Out of...?"

She reached for her bundle and peeled back a

corner of the blanket until a twist of brass gleamed. Folded back the next corner, and the next, until the full figure of the trumpet lay in her outstretched arms.

"No."

His answer was so swift and firm, but she stood her ground. Lifted her chin and hid the way his answer cut her. She held the instrument out further, waiting. Finally, he reached out to touch it.

He traced the small curve of the tuning slide, then on to the finger valves, letting his touch linger on the first, then the second...tapping lightly on the third and finally, carefully, compressing the formation to play an A.

Always together, she could almost hear her young voice, the moment she'd taught him how to push the two first buttons down side by side. *Like you and me.* She murmured those words aloud, and he withdrew from the trumpet as if it was already molten. "No," he said. "You can't melt that down."

"I can," she said. "It's mine. You know he gave it to me."

"No, you can't. And besides." He ran his hand over the dark scruff of the day shadowing his jaw. "It's not enough metal."

"I have more," she laughed. "Lots and lots more. A whole orchestra's worth." She watched the words do their work, the way he tipped his head to the side, looking from her, to the brass, and back again.

"Aria—" he said, then clamped his mouth shut around the name. "Miss St. John. Please. Take this. You can't melt that down." He pressed the trumpet into her arms. "Your father gave it to you. And that," he pointed at the instrument, "is someone's work of art."

He rolled the scroll back up, walked to the door and held it wide open. His message was clear: *leave.*

But she wouldn't budge. "Yes," she said. "He did. To play. And yes, it is someone's masterpiece, but..." she shook her head slowly, "they meant it to be played, too. And you and I both know that isn't possible. I mean to make something of these instruments." She held her arm fast around the trumpet, fingers stiff and slow as they tapped against it, demonstrating the old injury. "I will play them once more. In a different form."

He flinched. "But certainly not...for something like this," he shook his head. "You can't."

Aria lifted her chin, setting the trumpet back down. "I can't? Or you won't." She gestured at the canvas-covered table, then took measured steps toward him.

He averted his gaze, staring hard at the wall across the room, holding her scroll out to her. With her ever-gloved hands, she wrapped her fingers around his, pressing the scroll close in his palm and to his chest.

"At least think about it," she said. "Because James, I remember your work. What you used to do with this foundry, the metals you melted, the way you gave them new life... and yes. I'm crazy enough to turn my brass instruments into this," she tapped on the scroll, "but I can't do it without you." She pulled in a breath. "I wouldn't want to do it without you."

At last, he found her gaze. There was a hunger

there, a desperation for something—but quick as hope flickered, it was gone. "No." He slid his hands from beneath hers as if he could still feel the burn of them. As if her injuries hadn't been healed for years now. "Never again."

"Very well, then. You leave me no choice." She rummaged in her cape pocket, pulling out the token she'd carried with her from the island to boarding school and every day since. She'd needed it, the promise of it, to keep her going. And now, she needed it again. "You promised," she whispered. She placed it on the windowsill, and slipped out the door.

She couldn't bear to look back and see what those two words had done to him.

- CHAPTER 3 -

YOU PROMISED.

He had. James glared at the bronzed pebble on the windowsill.

Promises are for keeping, she'd told him once. He'd looked at her wide young eyes, at all that she, as a little girl, stood to accomplish in the world. A future like that...a girl of only eight years old who could play every instrument anyone could invent or imagine... he couldn't give her much, but he could give her a promise.

So he had. He'd made a sand mold for their favorite sea-plucked pebble and she'd watched him tamp it down, press it in, lift it out to leave its perfect impression.

He could almost see the longing on her face when he poured the bronze; she'd been begging and begging to try pouring herself. But he wouldn't let her. It was too dangerous.

When it was finished, he'd kept the stone and she'd kept the bronze-cast version of it. "Here," he said. "You keep this promise safe with you, I'll keep mine with me, and wherever you go, no matter what, I'll take care of you."

She'd wrapped her little fingers tight around it. Her fair face was solemn beneath freckle-splashed cheeks. "Promises are for keeping you know…"

He plucked her pebble up now, turning it in his palm. All these years later, she'd kept it. And now it was his turn. Except that there was the not-so-small matter of her father's warning.

The echo from the past fading around him, James strode over to the foundry, lifted the pebble he'd kept on her chair and studied it only to remember why he must never so much as touch the foundry again. With the pebble in one hand, her bronze replica of it in the other, he pressed his eyes shut. *God, forgive me.*

Before he could think twice, he set the pebbles side by side on the mantle and lifted the draped canvas from the foundry, a shower of dust choking the air. There it all was: the round form of the crucible, sand mold frames, implements to reshape and redeem hardened, impure metal into something new. The tools, once his old friends, now cruel reminders of how he'd single-handedly destroyed the ninth symphony of Giovanni St. John.

He unrolled Aria's scroll, placed the two stones on either end to keep the paper from furling, and took in what lay before him.

She was crazy. But then she'd always been this way—seeing possibilities that no one else would ever, in any lifetime, think of. On the paper before him, a cluster of instruments was sketched: trumpet, French horn, trombone, tuba. Then an arrow drawn from the cluster to what she wanted to make.

James clenched his jaw. What was she thinking? The instruments—the finest in the world, gifts from renowned artisans to her father, and from her father, to her... she wanted him to melt them. Into this.

A bicycle.

Well. If she wanted him to do this, she was going to have to explain herself a little more than her scribblings did. Granted, her "scribblings" were some of the finest, most precisely sketched plans he'd ever seen—down to the measurements, fittings, scale, part quantities— but still. He needed to know. Why in the world would she do that to those instruments? And for a bicycle, of all things.

A bicycle that he couldn't push out of his thoughts, try as he might. Not as he closed down the forge, not as he tromped up the stairs to bed, not even in his dreams.

When morning broke and he'd lit the first fire of the day to chase off the November chill, he set about business as usual: Put the kettle over the fire to cook his oats. Stoke the forging fire. Re-shroud the foundry, so he wouldn't have to look at it. And when he stood safe at last behind his forging bench, hammering away on Mr. Hathaway's garden gate, James began to feel a sense of normal once more. If he tried, he could almost ignore the lifeless foundry as he had every day before this. Ignore the carefully-sketched plans anchored down by the promise rocks, forget the girl who'd grown into a woman and upturned his universe last night.

Right on cue, she burst through the door. "I'm here to help!" Her cheeks were rosy and eyes alight with anticipation. No one ever came through his door with such delight, and certainly no one who tempted his gaze away from his work like she did. It was dangerous.

His hammering fell silent. He furrowed his brows.

"Come, now." She tucked emerald gloves beneath sleeves the same color. "It will be fine, James. Just like old times. And if we're to be done by

Christmas Eve…"

"Christmas Eve?" That was fast. For a project like this—too fast.

She nodded eagerly, a dark curl bouncing at her neck. "For the concert."

He laid down his mallet and clamped tongs around the scrolled piece. "I haven't said I'd do it."

She gave a quick glance at the weighed-down paper, and tilted her face in question. "Haven't you?"

He released the metal scroll, red with heat and new shape, into the tempering bucket. The air popped with the sizzle as it cooled, and he looked at Aria. The way she waited, that barely-contained spark of mischief in her eyes. He gave a deep sigh. He had, after all, made a promise.

But he'd given his word to her father, too. That he'd stay away from her. He swallowed, taking up another rod of black metal. "Aria…" he turned the rod in the fire, watching the black morph into its red glow. "Does your father know you're here?"

Her smile vanished. "Father sleeps most of the

day, now."

"So he doesn't know."

"He can't know, James. This is for him."

"Giovanni St. John is going to ride a bicycle." James knew he shouldn't be smiling at the thought, but he couldn't help it. The picture of the great composer, toddling about the island cliffs and farmland on a bicycle...

"It isn't funny, James!" She stepped so close he put an arm out to stop her.

"Careful," he said. "It's hot."

"I know what I'm doing." She shoved his arm away. "And no, Father is not going to ride it." She dropped her gaze to the floor between them.

"You're right," James said. "Because I can't do this. I'm sorry."

"But you must!"

James raised his mallet to deliver the first blow on the anvil. "I have to finish this gate, Aria. I'm sorry." It was only part of the reason, but it would have to do.

"Fine." Her skirt swished as she made her way

to the door and he was filled with an odd mingling of relief and disappointment. Until she reached for the broom in the corner instead of leaving, and started to work. She filled the room with a jaunty tune, humming as she swished cobwebs from the corner and swept the already-clean hearth three times.

James shook his head, covering a deep laugh with a fisted cough. The young woman standing before him was resolute beyond even the stubbornness of the little girl he knew.

She hummed her way through Greensleeves, whistled her way through Claire de Lune while fairly dancing with the broom, and on her third round of sweeping she started in on Christmas carols.

Christmas carols made James unreasonably angry when sung before December. ...and something in the way she kept glancing at him from beneath those long lashes told him that she remembered that little fact all too well.

He jabbed his tongs into the bucket to cool and folded his arms over his chest. "Alright." She kept singing. Wintry snowy words of yule that made him cringe.

"Alright," he repeated.

She stilled, resting the soft curve of her chin atop the broomstick. "What was that, Mr. Shaw?"

"I have something to take care of before I can say yes."

"Very satisfactory!" She said, and resumed her sweeping.

"You don't have to do that, you know." He pointed at the broom.

"Oh, I finish what I start, Mr. Shaw."

That's what he was afraid of. For what she'd begun, with this bicycle plan... he was afraid he'd have to tell her no, once and for all. But that would be up to Giovanni St. John.

Which meant James would have to face him. Tomorrow.

- CHAPTER 4 -

IF THE SILENT HOUSE had a heart, a single room that pumped life into every vein of its being, this would be it. The very spot where James stood, facing Giovanni St. John.

"You know where we are, of course." Aria's father spoke. No greeting. No eye contact. No acknowledgement that the last time they'd spoken, the man had sworn himself and his daughter away from this island forever. None of that. Just him, sitting on a stool in the center of the cavernous room, turning the peg of a violin ever-so-slowly. Yellow November sunlight shrouded the man from the arched windows beyond.

"Yes, sir." James knew where they were. Anyone would. An organ's pipes sprawled from wall to wall, shooting the height of the ceiling. The famed Broadwood—allegedly once Frederick Chopin's own grand piano—stood guard in the corner. And the empty glass baton case perched upon a lone white column beside Giovanni St. John.

James had never been allowed here, but he knew. This was the conservatory.

Giovanni turned the peg until the string was so tight it squeaked in protest. "I thought I'd see the channel freeze straight through before I ever saw you in this room." Bushy salt-and-pepper brows peaked, pinning him for an explanation.

James locked his own hands behind his back, ready for what was coming. The verbal lashing he knew he deserved.

"You remember these, of course," Giovanni gestured at the tuning pegs, beginning to twist the next in line. James remembered. "I had my doubts when they all said you were the one to commission for bespoke pieces. Something one-of-a-kind, as I needed. You were only a boy, after all. But then," this string squeaked, too, "I know a thing or two about child prodigies. I had my own one-person symphony here, once." He paused, and for the first time, looked at James. His face was tired. "But you know that."

James shuffled a foot. "Yes, sir. I do, sir. And please, you must know—"

Giovanni stood, matching James in height and levelling him with a stare. "This was crafted by Stradivari himself," he held the violin out to James. It was so small, just the size for a child to hold. Reluctantly, James took it, awash with fear that he'd destroy this, too.

"You did fine work on those tuning pegs, Mr. Shaw," Giovanni said.

James ran his fingers across the small gold pieces, remembering well the care he'd taken in casting each one, in engraving them with the letter *A*, afloat upon flourishes worthy of the talented little hands that played the instrument.

James swallowed. "Thank you, sir." He handed the violin back. This was torture. James braced himself. He wished Giovanni would just tell James exactly what he thought of him, let him hear the cruel truth once and for all. Or just punch him. Either would do.

But the man only ran his fingers down the strings of the neck one at a time, a voiceless dirge for what was lost.

"If I may, sir. I've come to ask your permission to—"

A deep cough rattled from Giovanni St. John, mingled with a laughter rolling with the bass of a tympani. "Don't tell me." He waved his coughing away, shoulders still quivering with laughter. "You haven't come to ask for her hand. Because the irony of that..." he shook his head.

Anger churned James's courage until it shot through him. No, he hadn't come to ask that. But how the man could joke like that about Aria's hands... he had to remind himself that the man was ill. Very ill, Aria had said. But that didn't excuse him from such an atrocity.

"No," James said. "I haven't." Not today, anyway. Though every moment that passed brought him closer to the thought.

"Good. You've done enough damage there."

James clamped his jaw tight. Took a deep breath. "I was wrong that day. I should never have let her—"

"'Let her'?" A dry laugh. "You're right. You should never have even let her through the door of your forge. She had no place there."

"And did she have any place spending every hour of every day kept up in this room? Working those hands over these instruments?" James had heard it, for five years or more. Tiny fingers, worked until her love for music was nearly worked right out of her. He pounded nails into mold frames, she strung bows over cellos, and their songs met in the street when they could not.

As soon as the words were out, though, James

regretted them. To speak so to a dying man… he stepped back, ready to leave. He'd save the man from pouring what fury he had left into putting James in his place.

He'd just have to tell Aria no. Help her find another way to do what she needed. Maybe he could persuade his brother John away from his farm and back into the forge long enough to help her.

James strode toward the French doors, but froze when he saw Giovanni's reflection in the glass. Shoulders slumped. Expression broken – just for a flash—but broken so deeply James turned to face him again.

"You swore to me you'd never go near her again," Giovanni said at last.

James braced himself. "Which is why I've come to ask your permission. To help her."

"With what?"

That, he could not say. It was Aria's secret to tell, not his.

Giovanni set his mouth in a grim line, any sign of

regret retreating again into his weathered features. "I see," he said. He set the violin down on the chair and strode in measured steps to the white column pedestal. He lifted the lid of the empty glass baton case, stared inside.

James couldn't take it. He had to speak up, assure him he'd never hurt Aria again, and would do anything to take back the irreparable damage of that day. "With respect, Sir, if I may—"

"She's lost much, Mr. Shaw." He closed the lid abruptly, its solid click echoing with finality. He ran a finger along the edge of the lid. "I don't deny that I..." Something was so close, so ready to be spoken. He cleared his throat, shook the almost-spoken words away. "Just see that she doesn't lose more. That's all that I ask."

Judging by his stance, the interview was over. And one did not argue with Giovanni St. John.

James gripped the cold, scrolling door handle—his own father's handiwork. But one last look at the mighty composer walking so slowly toward the window, surrounded by his own museum of instruments, and he knew he might never have this chance again.

"Mr. St. John?" He shouldn't be speaking. He knew it. But he couldn't help it. He swallowed. "I'm sorry."

The man paused long enough to half-turn his head. And nod.

"For everything," James said. "I never meant any harm to come to her."

A pause. "I know."

"I'd do anything for her."

Giovanni turned to face him full on, now, the sunlight silhouetting him. "Well. Why don't you start by helping her with whatever it is she's got rolled up in that scroll of hers? She thinks I don't see her go traipsing over to your forge. She thinks she's keeping some secret. And I won't pry it out of her before she's ready. But understand this. If she needs your help... you help her."

A chasm opened in James then, freedom

surging through him. "Yes, Sir!" Never were two words meant more.

At last, he would make this right. And maybe... just maybe... he would find a way to give Aria her music back, too.

- CHAPTER 5 -

THE NEXT DAY, James chased concentration relentlessly. When Aria didn't burst through the door like she had two days before, he set to work on Mr. Hathaway's hinges. When she still hadn't appeared an hour later, he tried a whistle a tune to fill the silence, cringing at the flat way it fell around him.

"You're a fool, James Shaw," he muttered. He was a fool for looking at the door every fifteen minutes, willing it to open. And a fool for bungling the hinges not once, not twice, but three times.

By late afternoon, weary of the tedious day, he almost let out an audible *thank goodness* when Aria's rosy face appeared at his window beside him. She knocked, tipped her head to the side in question and held up a picnic basket fringed in red plaid. "Time for tea?" she said, voice muted through the steamed glass.

What a sight they must have made walking together, she in her ruffled grey dress and carefully-coiled hair, he in his plain black trousers and working coat, cap thrown on as a last-minute defense against the cold. They headed away from the village, through the aspen grove. The islanders, who had an infamous way of making mountains of molehills, liked to call this the "woods."

"Remember when we tried to get lost in the woods?" Aria gave him a wry smile.

James laughed. Yes, he remembered it. Very well. "It was a challenge," he said. Forty trees, at the very most, stood in bare winter white. "Let's see, we tried blindfolding ourselves, walking backwards, standing on our heads."

Aria laughed, her voice like a song. "But it wasn't until we spun around twelve times a piece that we managed to get lost."

"Well..." James remembered Aria's seven-year-old delight at finally getting lost in the woods. He remembered he couldn't bring himself to tell her he knew exactly where they were—that the rock tunnel lay just meters to their left, that the bluebells grew just a jaunt to their right.

"James Shaw." Aria halted, mouth open, fist on her hip. "Don't tell me you weren't lost."

"Alright," he said. "I won't."

She shrieked, then gathered her skirt to chase him. All the way to the dune they ran, the years of separation flying away on the sharp wind. Finally, they stopped at Trouble Cliff to catch their breath. It was a singular place—the island's own personal Stonehenge of sorts. Rock pillars, moved there by nobody-knew-who, a century or more before, stood all in a row to mark the sheer drop into the ocean.

"Lovely day for a picnic," Aria said, tossing a dimpled look of amusement over her scarlet cape. She rummaged in the basket for the blanket.

Heavy white clouds pushed in from the North. "Indeed," James said, matching her wit with dry gravity. "I'd count on snow tonight."

"We'll make the best of our picnic, then." Flinging the red woolen blanket up and out, she laughed as it tangled in the wind. James retrieved the far corners, spreading it out, and soon they were communing over still-warm scones from the kitchen of the Silent House.

"Father says you paid him a visit?" Aria raked swirling patterns into the sand beside her with her fingers.

James chewed slowly, taking his time before he answered. "I did. I needed to ask him something."

"But you kept the secret." Aria peaked a brow.

"Of course."

"So we'll start tomorrow?"

They should. There was his promise to her. There was the fact that the indomitable Giovanni St. John had just told him to help her. There was the Christmas Eve deadline to be met. And yet... there was something amiss here, a thought he'd been circling all night and all day. James shook his head. "The bicycle. It's an amazing thought, Aria." Hesitancy lined his voice.

She bristled.

"...but?"

James tossed a grey pebble, sent it flying over the sheer drop beyond them. "Nothing."

"Maybe I don't know you like I once did, James, but I can still tell when you're not saying something."

"I just...from the time I can remember, I was making things for you." His dark eyes flicked to the side, out over the sea where the wind beat waves beat on the rocks below. "For your music. And I know what happened took that from you, but I just can't help thinking, there must be a way to give that back to you."

She sat up straight, a deep pain playing across her face. "You think I gave up too quickly?"

No, James wanted to shout. That wasn't what he meant at all. But there had to be a way. Something he could do to give her back her music. How could he possibly put into words... *Please, God.* If he could just make her understand, just make her see how he wanted to fight for her—

But Aria was backing away, fire in her eyes. "You have no idea." She sucked in a breath. "You have no right... you have no idea what it took to let go, James."

"Aria, there was no one like you. There *is* no one like you. Maybe you didn't have a choice in learning all those instruments, but who else in this whole world could have done it like you did? Your music filled this whole island. And if you'll let me, I will find a way."

"Listen." The wind pulled dark strands of hair loose, whipping them about her face. "I am never going to have the strength in my hands that I once did. It's irreparable." She held up her stiff fingers as if to prove her point. "And that is my fault."

Now that, James could not tolerate. She, blaming herself, when he was the one... "No, it's—"

"Don't think Father didn't try to fix it. Don't think I haven't been to every specialist on the continent, every surgeon in England." She shook her head. "They say the damage ran too deep, the scars are too extensive."

"I'm sorry," he said, taking that hand in his. Wishing he could take the damage from her, bear it himself, until the weight of the desire squeezed the air from him. "I should have been there."

She stepped back. "No." She was quiet, but steel surrounded her tone. "There is nothing to be sorry for. Yes, they say the scars are too extensive, but scars are places made strong again. They don't function like they did before, but they're strong for something. Something that matters. And I am choosing to be strong for this, James. Because if Father will never hear his ninth symphony again... at least he'll see it play. I can do that. I will."

With that, she clutched her basket and strode back to the village, leaving James with more regret than ever.

Aria wrapped a third blanket around herself that night, teeth chattering in the dark as she pulled back her father's heavy velvet bed curtain to check on him. It wasn't snow that had come tonight, as James had mused. Just a coldness so dry and fierce it crackled against the windowpanes of Father's bedchamber. One of the many things James had been wrong about today.

Father lay so still, Aria's knees almost buckled at the sight of him. But there—she spotted a tiny exhale escape his mouth, a white cloud against the frigid air. And another after that. Shallow and raw each breath came, steady enough that she found her own strength once again.

He'd sat up far too late after his rehearsal with the small orchestra at the church. She'd known he needed rest, but he seemed so alive, telling her about the way the farmer played the violin without a bow, and how a boy had come in late for rehearsal, smelling of salt air and fish, and piping out the clearest tune he'd ever heard on a fife. "This may be my greatest performance yet, Aria," he'd said. "But the cellist needs rosin. His bow sounds like a deplorable screeching cat. And I need to transcribe a few things..." he'd rattled on, handing a list to their manservant and insisting that Barnes take the evening steamer to Guernsey for supplies.

But now here Father lay, even his heavy bed curtains doing little to keep any warmth in. He was so cold...

Aria fed the last log into his fire, then took herself downstairs. What a fool she was. No more wood in the house, and the coldest part of the night yet upon them. If she'd sent word for more wood yesterday, as she'd meant to. But then she'd gotten carried away with her bicycle plans and forgotten.

There was only one place she could think to find ready-cut wood this time of night. The warmest place on the island...and it mattered not that the man inside was the last person she wanted to talk to right now. Father needed firewood, and that was that. She took herself across the green, shivering beneath her thin shawl.

In hushed tones, she explained to the bed-tousled blacksmith, trying hard not to notice the dark circles beneath his blue eyes, or the way he started gathering logs from his own stack before she'd even finished talking. Trying not to wonder why he'd answered his door before she'd knocked even three times.

She followed him back to the Silent House, fairly running to keep up with his long strides, and led the way to Father's bedchamber. She passed him dry twigs for kindling and with deft hand he coaxed the embers into a fire so toasty the room warmed in minutes. Before she could thank him, he was out the door, across the green, and back again with a second armload of wood. Despite his hushed protests she took to stacking it, and he vanished for a third trip.

By then, Aria was losing her resolve to resent his words earlier that day. Somewhere between his second and third trip, she found herself below stairs in the kitchen, warming milk delivered from Spencer's dairy farm that day, melting rough-cut chunks of chocolate into it. She carried a pot and two cups up into the dark hall and followed the echoing sounds until she found him at work in the sitting room, laying a fire there.

One look at what she carried and he was swift to take it from her, place it on the hearth. "You shouldn't be carrying that," he said, but when his eyes met hers, she saw he regretted the words.

She poured a cup of cocoa for him, and one for herself, while he moved to examine the ornately carved mahogany cabinet in the corner. "How does this work?" His brows furrowed in that curious concentration that sometimes captured him.

She carried a mug over and handed it to him, then pulled the glass door of the cabinet open. "Listen," she said, and pulled a metal disc out. Placing the disc inside the cabinet so that it faced them, she released the machine to do its work as it slowly moved the disc around, releasing the warmth of a jingly melody into the room.

James's expression broke into wonder. "A music box?"

Tiny indentations traversed the large disc, catching the tines beneath it as they passed over. "You just place whichever disc you'd like to hear upon it," she said. "It's years since I've heard one like this play, though." The light measures filled the room until the disc had turned its full revolution. Aria stopped the machine and motioned to the chair nearest the fire, for him to sit.

James leaned forward, propping his elbows upon his knees while he turned the mug in his hands. At length, he finally spoke. "I'm sorry, Aria. I shouldn't have said that just now."

"...said what?" She moved to the chair opposite his, and took a sip from her cup. Warm and rich.

"About carrying the hot teapot... and about your music. Earlier, I mean. On the cliff."

She shook her head. "I'm the one who's sorry, James. I spoke harshly today."

"You had every right to."

"No. Not to you. Not like that."

"I'm glad you said what you did," he narrowed his eyes as he studied the fire in the hearth. "I want to understand. And I want to help."

Aria considered his position. What must the past few days have been like for him? Minding his business, gentling metal into function and art and holding this island together the way he did so faithfully with each creation, large or small. From the ornate gates in front of the old ruins, to humble horseshoes that kept every farm working. And then in she blew, turning it all topsy-turvy and dredging up a time he'd doubtless rather forget. Yet here he was, looking at her with such a gentle hunger in his eyes, waiting to receive whatever story she might tell. He deserved an explanation.

"Last summer," she began, "I was in Lyon. I learned of a bicycle race a man had decided to put on. A promotion for his newspaper, but it was unlike any other race in the whole world. The Tour de France, they called it."

Even thinking of it sent such a jolt of excitement through her. "The things those men did, James. Cycling through the night, hundreds of miles at a time...they were hungry, thirsty, tired... in pain..." she shook her head. "It was incredible. Insane, but incredible. I saw them pass through and if you could've watched the determination on their faces...the absolute grit. There was one man—the Little Chimney Sweep, they called him. That's what he used to do, sweep chimneys. But here he was, leading the entire pack of professional racers on a machine he once spent his days admiring from rooftops."

James nodded kindly, though a shadow of confusion fell over him.

She must sound like a fool, chattering on about a bicycle race. "Days and days—weeks! of cycling and when they finally rode into Paris to the finish line—guess who was at the front of the pack. Guess who won the whole race."

James let his mouth stretch into that slow smile of his. "The chimney sweep?"

Aria jumped in her seat, nearly sloshing her sipping chocolate all over her lap. "Yes! The Little Chimney Sweep! I kept thinking about him. For years, he climbed roofs, descended ladders. Up and down over the city, every day. But he dared to think of a different way of living. Forward-moving. The very same muscles, but used in a different way."

James sat up taller, then stood, placing his mug atop the hearth and taking up the poker. "Like your instruments," he said.

Aria drew in a deep breath. To be understood... there was no joy like it. "Exactly. I had thought I'd seen the end of them. I asked Father once if we could donate them perhaps, but he wouldn't. Or couldn't. I'm not certain which. He offered funds to donate new instruments instead. I just don't think he's ever given up hope that one day I might play them again. I'd thought they'd live here always, abandoned, with only the occasional cleaning Father orders for the house... but that's when I got the idea for the bicycle."

"The instruments could have a different sort of

movement," James said with a thoughtful nod, poking a log and setting off a spray of sparks.

"And life!" Aria hopped up, joined him at the hearth.

"And," James held her gaze, reached out to press a strand of her hair between his fingers. "The ninth symphony would have a way of playing."

She swallowed. Hearing those words spoken quickened her nerves so. "Yes," she said, sobering. "There is a verse," she closed her eyes, recalling the words. "*The Lord is my strength and song, and is become my salvation.* Those first years, after the accident, those words were my lifeline. I had no strength, I had no song. At least I thought I didn't. But songs are more than music."

James nodded, and she continued. "When I look at this chance—I can't help thinking, maybe this gift for my father— I could be strong for *that*. That whatever is laid before us to do, that is our song." She stepped close to James, slipping her hand inside of his, feeling his warmth around her. "Right now, this project is what's been put before me. Will you help me?"

With a gentle squeeze of his fingers, the dawning of joy in his eyes, she had her answer.

- C H A P T E R 6 -

"ON ONE CONDITION." James instructed the next morning. "I'll do the casting. You," he pointed to the clear area of the workshop—the safe place. Near the table. Far from where the molten metal would be. "Chalk the design full-scale on the floor there. And only there. We'll need it to lay the pieces out on." And if she would only stay there, James told himself, he could justify allowing her in again. "And you're so much better with the scale drawings than I am," he said. She'd always been sharp with numbers.

She grinned. "Fair enough." Rubbing her gloved

hands together, wrapped in their island-knit wool. She glanced around. "Where's the chalk?"

Despite his best efforts to the contrary, a chuckle slipped out at her eagerness. "Just there," he pointed to the mantle, then plucked up the trumpet, ready to disassemble and melt. "You realize this will be the heaviest bicycle known to man," he said.

She nodded, eyes alight. "That doesn't matter," she said.

"And you realize it could take weeks to do this."

"Of course," she said. "But I know we can have it done in time. Can't we?" a pleading look settled into her features.

James glanced at the calendar. Christmas Eve was five weeks away. It would be tight, with all of his other projects to do as well... but there were nights, too, if days ran short, and he'd gladly forgo sleep to make this happen. Especially with the idea he had brewing... but it wasn't time to share that with her just yet.

"Yes. We can do it. Christmas Eve shall have its

bicycle."

With that, the first brick in a wall a decade thick between them crumbled. And day by day, bits of that wall fell, light slipping in through each new chink.

There was the day he forced himself to subject that first trumpet to the fires of the foundry. Aria stole close to him to watch as the metal glowed white beneath the dross.

"We'll remove that?" she asked, pointing at the dark matter.

James took a ladle and drew the dross with a stir, lifting it out. He let Aria linger there only long enough for him to see the delight glowing in her, then he tipped his head back toward the hearth, where her chalk waited.

But he kept looking up to catch her staring at him. Just as quick, she'd look away, and just as quick, he'd make himself break his stare, too. There was something new in her gaze, and more present each time. Something that made him stand a little straighter as he worked.

A week later, on the last day of November, she traipsed in with a wreath. Without even asking, dragged a stepladder toward the mantle to hang it up.

And then the Christmas carols started again. He tried, he really tried, to lift his hard-and-fast hatred of festivities before December. It was so close, after all. Mere hours, really. But they were so wretchedly jolly, James could barely stand it.

Until she opened her mouth and, in that pure and airy soprano, began the soft strains of *Silent Night*. It wrapped him, the melody did, and held him fast. On she sang until she reached the fourth verse: *With the dawn of redeeming grace...*

She stopped abruptly, and tipped her head as if listening.

"The dawn of redeeming grace." She picked up with the song again, repeating that line more slowly. The way she spoke the words made him think of the way she looked on their beach-treasure expeditions, turning each rock over looking for something of great worth.

Her tune carried on, Aria piecing the bicycle parts together with a deep concentration as the words faded into a hum. When she finally stopped, the air hung with those repeated words and he found he didn't mind the way they lingered. Didn't mind one bit.

Then, there was the day when the familiar clanking and tapping and etching of her work fell still. Worried, James sat forward from his stool in order to see her where she sat, skirts billowed in blue around her, studying him with an intensity that made him sit up straight.

He swiped at his forehead, as if the motion could dispel the flush of heat across his face. Finally, he stilled his hammer and fixed her with a stare right back. He could win a staring contest, this they both knew. "Well?" he said.

"The molds," she said, at his side in a heartbeat. She reached into the wooden box to touch the sand mixture, packed so firmly around the wheel indentation. "I'd forgotten how you set these." She traced her finger lightly along the imprint, where molten brass would soon flow—

And that's when he saw. She wore no gloves. For the first time since the day she'd stepped back over his threshold, there were her scars.

Only for an instant did he allow himself to look. But they drew him. They tied her to him, forever marked her with his carelessness.

Swiftly, she pulled her hand back into the shadows of her skirts and stepped back. Just as quickly, he reached for his hammer to resume his light tapping, but he could feel the warmth of her continued study of him.

"Does it..." James kept hammering, ever-lighter with each word he spoke, stealing glances at her. "Does it hurt?"

She pursed her lips, glancing out the window, to the ground, and finally at her hands, running her fingers around the arm that bore the most markings.

"No," she said quietly. "Not anymore."

He recalled her father's words: *She's already lost so much...*

"Father sees me now, you know." She said, her skirts swishing as she moved to hand him a nail. He took it, listening. "Before... he heard me. But he never saw me. Not really."

"...and now?"

"Now I can't be his loophole in that silly superstition any longer. As long as that's what I was...that was *all* I was." her voice trailed off and she shook her head. "Anyway. He's changed. When we talk in the evenings now, he listens. All his life, the world has been clamoring to listen to him. And he thrived on it. But now—there is this quiet in him, when he looks at me, when he asks me about my time at boarding school all those years. In any case," she summoned a cheeriness back into her voice, "I want to do this for him."

Slowly, she retreated back to her work, and James resumed his hammering with renewed fervor.

"We're almost there, Aria," he said, so low he wasn't sure she heard.

Finally, the crowning day came. After weeks of melting, pouring, molding, hammering, polishing, studying, casting, recasting every single pipe, gear, pin… today was the day. Today, they'd shape the handlebars and put the last of the pieces together.

Everything was perfect. Until Aria drew up next to him, such a look of longing on her face. "Can I pour?"

He slammed his hammer toward the mold nail, missing completely and scarring the wood.

No. The word pounded in his head but wouldn't make it past his tongue. He pleaded it instead silently, and he saw mirrored in her face the ache of what he'd done to her eight-year-old self.

"It wasn't your fault, James."

A dry laugh scraped through his throat, audible regret. "No? Who else could have kept you safe that day? Kept you—"

Her hand was on his arm, bearing only gentleness. "It was my idea."

"Yes, and you were eight. It was my responsibility."

"You were *ten*." She let that small word linger. "Ten. We were having one of our larks, that's all. One of the only shreds of light in my life back then, by the by."

He glanced at the promise rocks, the lantern behind them flinging great shadows from their small forms. "But... I promised," he strode to the mantel and picked up her bronze-cast rock. Please." He pleaded with his eyes. "Do not go near the foundry."

She looked as crushed as she used to when they were young and he wouldn't allow her near the crucible. And it was almost enough to change his mind. But no. Never again would he risk her to the flame. Not when they were this close to giving the symphony its unlikely voice, at last.

- CHAPTER 7 -

ARIA KNEW SHE SHOULDN'T have asked to pour the metal.

But to be a part of this transformation... oh, she'd give anything if he'd just let her try. She plucked her way around the parts on the floor. To anyone other than her and James, the arrangement would look a mess—a graveyard for brass bicycle parts, of all things. But she knew just how each piece fit with the next.

As the two of them worked, the distance between them yawned greater even as the room squeezed smaller. At length James rose and moved to sit beside her, taking the crosspiece from her hands and laying it aside with a gentle click against the stone floor. Slowly, he reached for her hand... gloved, once again. She let him, but wouldn't meet his gaze.

Silence pulsed louder every second that passed. If she could somehow make him understand...

"You're still the only one who knows," she said. "About the ninth, I mean. And me. I mean about the ninth and me and..." she pursed her lips, leaving the rest unsaid.

He covered her hand with his free one. They sat that way, fire crackling behind them and the past and future melding right there. This quiet between them was safe and full, something she didn't have the heart to break by speaking of that day so long ago. Lifting a large plate of notched brass for one of the gears, she watched the reflection: James's quiet presence, leaning forward to take hold of bicycle parts, continue his work while just sitting with her. Maybe he sensed the gift of this shared quiet, too. Maybe he was remembering that day, too. Her own reflection looked in some ways a stranger—but perhaps, somewhere in her features, there still lay a bit of that music-filled soul she'd been, once upon a time.

Closing her eyes, Aria let the steady sounds of James working beside her carry her back to that day...

Aria. Even her name spoke the purpose of her life: a song. A symphony. She didn't mind, really... she loved the music. The way she could place her lips to a reed, stretch her little eight-year-old fingers just so and make, out of nothing, a note fill the room. But what she really liked was the way her father's stern countenance softened— ever-so—when he listened to her play. The way he told her sometimes that she was the only living symphony there ever was or ever would be—his ninth. The only symphony that didn't have to be written, because she lived music.

The violin. The trumpet. The flute, the lyre. Woodwinds, brass, and strings—she was every part the orchestra, and the orchestra was every part of her. But still, there was something in Father that she couldn't reach. A hunger, and she wanted to make it alright. Perhaps if she could give him a gift. Just for him. James had made her that rock... could she make something like that for Father? She could think of only one thing that meant the world to him.

On the eve of her ninth birthday, she waited until her father had gone out, then sneaked into his conservatory to remove his special baton from its glass case. Five minutes later, she was knocking on the door of the forge. Their secret knock, so James would know it was her. But no one answered.

It was alright. She'd seen him do this a thousand times. And, everyone on the island said, James was equal in talent to his father and brothers, even at his young age. Some said he was even better. She found his gloves and put them on, giggling at the way they swallowed her small hands whole. James wouldn't mind if she used the foundry. It was ready. Or if she used some of the brass scraps from his scrap shelf. He wouldn't mind, she told herself again and again: when she stirred the metal, pulled out the dross, dipped in Father's conducting baton. Oh, how pleased he would be! To see it shine! He was just finished writing his tenth symphony—and now, when he conducted, he would have a proper baton. From her. His symphony girl. And maybe he would remember her because of it, everywhere he went, always in every symphony, even if he'd said she had to stay here on the island.

James would be proud, too, for the way she'd done this herself. One more dip of the baton and she pulled it out, held it out to watch the metal as it gleamed and cooled. At last, she set it down, peeled off the gloves, and turned to go.

But at the door, she stopped. She'd forgotten to remove the rest of the molten brass. What if James needed the crucible for something else? She must make it ready, just-so, for him. With deft speed and care, she stole back to the foundry and began to ladle it back out.

She was too small to pick up the heavy cylinder and pour it into the ingot molds. But she could scoop it. Once, twice...

And then the door creaked wide open behind her and she'd never heard such alarm as she did in James's voice. Two little words-- "Aria, no!"—a startled jump, and that was all it took. A tiny stumble backward, a collision with the table behind her, the spilling of the ladle down over her fingers, her arms. Splattered pain so deep she could not even cry. Could not feel. Could only work to find breath as she watched James run for her, the world slowing suddenly before her.

She shook her head in frantic protest as she watched her father's baton roll, brass and all, straight into the coals of the fire.

On the eve of her ninth birthday, the Secret Symphony of Giovanni St. John fell silent.

"Aria," James's voice was steady beside her, pulling her out of the memory and into a moment that felt like home. He spoke her name like he held a secret that might harm her. "Tell me... if you could play again... would you?"

That was a question she dared not answer.

- CHAPTER 8 -

WITH THE SUN BARELY CRESTING the thatched rooftops of the village the next morning, Aria slipped through spears of white morning dawn. Light touched the frosted world, setting everything aglow. Sleeping grass, crisp beneath her feet, carried her swiftly to her Blacksmith.

But he was not there.

No fire in the hearth, no coals in the forge, no sign of life anywhere but the frosty breath in front of her own face.

"James?"

Silence.

"Ja-ames," she called, trying to keep her voice light. The warmest place on the island was as cold as ice. Abandoned. And her bicycle... was gone.

Back outside she ran, down the cobbled street. Past the bakery where the smell of sweet rolls blew like a gale when the door opened as she passed by. She collided straight into strong arms, scrambling to find her footing.

"Slow down," James chuckled, brushing the loose strands of hair from her face. His smile vanished, though, and he must have read the panic on her face for his voice grew grave. "What is it?"

"You."

"Me?"

"Missing," she gasped to catch her breath.

"I'm here," he said, serious still.

Yes, he was. Dark lashes framing blue eyes that flustered her frightfully in the way they beheld her.

"I mean the—" a quick look around showed her it was safe to speak the secret, but she whispered it still.

"The bicycle is missing."

"Ah," James said, mirth pulling his smile into that slow warmth of his. He leaned forward conspiratorially. "Follow me."

He led her to the stone outbuilding behind the forge, a place that had always housed the forge's supplies. But as James dashed toward the weathered red door, a boyish look of eagerness on his face, Aria suspected something more than iron and coal was hidden inside.

She stepped into the room, shrouded in a sacred quiet. An oversized desk was pushed up against the solitary window, wood-topped in warm dark tones, with legs of slowly wandering iron scrolls holding it up. Lanterns hung on either side of the window, tiny lights splashing shadows down along with the morning sun.

The whole room ushered her in with its warmth from a small stove in the corner. And in the corner opposite stood a sight that had Aria blinking back tears—the gleaming brass bicycle. Assembled and nearly ready to go. She'd seen it before, of course, but almost every bit of it was there now, from spokes to wheels. All but the handlebars.

Aria cleared her throat, trying to compose herself. With another glance around the room, she gave James a quizzical look. "A bit different here now, isn't it?"

James beamed. "When my father asked me to take over the forge, he did this for me. He said it was a place to think, that everyone needed a place to think. Come," James gestured toward the desk and pulled out the wooden chair for her. "I've something to show you."

From a small drawer, James pulled a folded paper. He held it in both hands and shifted slightly. Why was he so nervous? It was rather endearing, but he was so serious, Aria stifled a smile.

"You might not like this," he said, unfolding it corner by corner. "And... it's alright if you don't. But if you do, I mean, that is—if you'd rather—"

She grew serious too, now, watching the way whatever that paper held pulled at him. She nudged her chair to the left, making room as he bent nearer, so close his jacket pressed against her ever-so-slightly.

He placed the paper before her and smoothed it out. His eyes narrowed in a study of the diagram before them, the same way he'd taken in her bicycle sketch that first night.

Quickly, Aria shifted her gaze to the diagram. She could feel every piece of the sketch—from the ruler-straight lines to each of James's notes written in such slanted, stiff characters—all of it flying from the paper to her mind as she pieced it together.

"It's...an attachment," he blurted. "For the bicycle." A wavering hope threaded through his words.

She didn't look at him. Only stood, paper still in hand, and paced in front of the fire. At one point she stopped, ran a finger beneath his notes, and shook her head, trying to take it in.

"I know," James said, hanging his head. "It's...not... maybe it's..."

"Amazing." Aria whispered the word, and fixed her eyes on the man who'd thought of this.

"I know it might not even work," he winced, "but if you'll look at the diagram you'll see there's a way we can fit the disc so that it won't—wait. Did you say..."

"Amazing, James. This," she held the paper up, an excitement breaking through her entire being, "is brilliant. How did you ever think of such a thing? A music box! Or not a box at all really—but a music apparatus? To be played by the wheel as it's pedaled..." she shook her head again and joy traversed James's face. What would it mean to Father, to hear notes from her, just one last time?

Raking his fingers through his hair, James took up her pacing where she'd left off. "So the disc indentations will catch the tines," he was muttering now. "When the wheel revolves... see?" He was beside her, holding one end of the paper as she held the other. "We'll take the workings of a disc music box and mount it—and then cast a disc for your song..." he scratched his head. "You wouldn't know where we might find one... would you?" Mischief twinkled in his words. "Because if you do, I can ensure it's put back to rights later."

Aria laughed at his eagerness. "I know just where to find one." She shook her head in wonder, hand resting at her throat. Her eyes travelled to the short bars of music at the bottom of the page. That he'd thought of this song, even...

The idea of it filled her. Just little bumps, catching metal tines. Disruptions on their own, but spaced perfectly to span these four measures-- the injuries to the smooth metal would make a song. A perfect one.

Now if only James would let her be the one to pour the molten brass to create the disc...perhaps it was silly, but she longed to touch, to pour, to be a part of the transformation.

"Could we really make a proper disc for the music player out of it? It's a simple song, I know, but can we do it?"

"We can," he said, determination so strong in his voice she could feel it. Aria followed as James led the way back toward the forge. "And we will."

James was so thankful, his steps fairly pounded with it. As he kindled the foundry for the last bits of brass they'd need to pour the music disc, he watched Aria move about the forge, so at home here he couldn't imagine it without her. She was quiet as she swept, no whistling or humming now. But every now and again she'd stop her sweeping and just look at him, wonder written in her lovely features.

So she didn't despise him, then. She very well could have, and had every right to.

"I'll be back soon," James said. "I'm going to finish the handlebars—I left the pipe for them outside overnight to freeze."

"To...freeze?" Her laughter spilled forth,

glowing warmer than all the embers he'd ever stoked.

"It doesn't sound right, does it? But the ice inside braces it, so it won't be crushed during the bending."

Aria seemed to let those words sink in, then gave a little wave.

"I'll be back soon," James said. His heavy boots carried him to the door, where he paused. She was just so quiet. Foreboding concern washed through him. "Are you alright?"

She nodded vigorously. "Never better," she said. Gathering the broom close, she drew herself up and gave a playful shooing motion out the door. But one last glance over his shoulder and he caught the tiny step she took toward the foundry, where fire burned deep inside. Just as quickly though, she resumed her sweeping.

James crunched over frost-glazed ground to the side of the stone building. Steps firm with purpose, he gripped the frozen pipe, taking care as he pulled, pounded, and bent it around his shaping cylinder. First one way, then the other, as the sharp break of ice crackled inside. And as he turned each curve, a thought began to dawn. Tomorrow, Aria would grasp hold of these bars. This chance she'd given him—perhaps it was unintentional, but somehow it seemed to matter—she'd given him the chance to place music right back into her hands.

The sharp air filled his chest with a new hope. A few more taps, a turn or two more... and the handlebars were done. Finished. Ready for her to--

He froze, one foot through the door. She stood at the foundry. Arms at her sides, but so close—he could see the effort it was taking her not to reach for the ladle, dip it in.

Aria, no!

His mouth moved to form the words but something stopped him. A scene in his memory flooding back, his ten-year-old-self causing the injury he'd been desperate to prevent with those very words.

It was as if the cold from the handlebars seeped into his bones, spread through his body and he moved with the slow restraint of the frozen brass wrapping its cold grip around the shaping cylinder. Steady. He set the handlebars down and felt the frost in his bones dissolve into the warmth of the room. Hand sliding around her ungloved one, he meant to stop her. To still those arms and keep his promise.

But then she turned her head, those dark curls brushing just beneath his chin and such a yearning in her eyes...

"James..." a score of pleading notes burned between them in that one word. But something changed in that instant—all questions etched in the curves of her face, replaced by something deeper still. She raised those silent fingers to trace his jaw as she spoke. "It's alright," she said. A step away from her foundry. A step toward him. "Thank you...for keeping your promise."

The promise to take care of her. Yes. That was right ...wasn't it? Keep her away from what burned her, what took the music from her. Keep her safe. But deep down, he knew there was more to this. Who was he protecting, really, by keeping her from the crucible?

Slowly, she moved toward the door. There she paused, and a sad smile settled over her. Before he could burst from this steel cage around him, she was gone.

- CHAPTER 9 -

"ONE DAY MORE, FATHER." Aria tied the last crimson ribbon on their tree, thankful for the way its height covered the conspicuously blank wall behind it. "And Christmas Eve is upon us."

"Yes," a slow laugh crawled through his words. "And I will conduct the infamous Treble-Clef-Upon-Trouble-Cliff." He shook his head. "I never imagined this would be my finale, Aria."

She lowered herself to the floor beside his chair, taking his hand. "What did you imagine?"

He closed his eyes, and she could almost feel his remembering. "It doesn't matter," he said at length, and squeezed her hand back. "This is better."

Oh, she hoped it would be. If they could make the disc work with the music box attachment on the back wheel of the bicycle as it turned... but she didn't know, now, whether they'd be done in time.

That night, as she tamed and braided her long hair, she tried to ignore the way the unlit candle in her window called to her. *Light me*, it seemed to say. But she couldn't. She turned back the bed sheets, shivered and hopped inside. And as she closed her eyes and turned her back against the window, she willed sleep to come...

But it would not. Silly as it was, she wrapped her blanket around her and answered the call of the candle. Nothing made sense in lighting it. The blacksmith shop windows were dark. James likely wouldn't see it. He hadn't lit his in answer to hers last time she'd tried this. She'd seen the way he'd withdrawn into himself this afternoon, and she didn't want to force him to re-live that day. But perhaps if he did see her candle... she could speak her remorse. Scrape away the dross of that guilt once and for all.

Aria retrieved a long match from her mantle, bent to light it in the embers of her fireplace, and cupped her free hand in front of the small flame. But when she arrived back at the window, a tiny movement across the green took her breath away. A light, rising and falling with the swing of a man's stride.

In the middle of the green he stopped, raising his lantern in silent invitation for her:

Meet me at the dune.

Her nerves washed wild with the sight, the hope of it. She shook her match out, pulled on her boots, and took the stairs two at a time while struggling into her overcoat.

Out in the night, James was gone. The cold didn't even register as she stole through the village, but for the way her breath puffed quick clouds into the air. Everything was a blur beneath the dark canvas of the sky, perfectly pin-pricked with starlight. Through the rock tunnel she went, and swiftly through the woods, following the path to their dune where she saw the soft glow of a beach fire, nestled into a clearing among the grasses. And beside it, James.

He was stirring something. Was that—she drew near to be sure her eyes weren't deceiving her—the crucible?

Spotting her, James closed the gap between them swiftly, taking her cold hand in his warm one. "You came," he said.

"Of course I came." She swallowed hard, as if that could contain the surge in her chest she felt in his firelight presence. In the way gentle lines framed his smile.

A quick glance at the crucible, and he led her toward it. "This is for you," he said, gesturing toward it. "Brass, ready to be made into the disc that will play your song."

Her breath hitched. "Really?"

He took her hand. "Yes. I should never have stood in your way."

"No," she said. "I shouldn't have asked you that. I should never have touched your crucible the day of the accident—I knew I wasn't supposed to. It was my fault, and I need to ask your forgiveness."

"I'm the one who needs forgiving, Aria," his voice was hoarse.

She pressed her fingers tight as she could around his as the cold of the night pulled around them. "All is well," she said.

"All is well," he repeated. Letting his hand linger on hers, he guided her toward the ladle that lay on a rock in waiting. Together, they raised it above the glow of white brass. The color of things pure and new. With a single word—"ready?"—he stepped slowly away from her.

And suddenly, there beneath that clear night sky, it was just Aria and the silenced music, fluid and flowing in a dance of re-shaping.

As she poured, she could hear the metal making its way down the carefully-placed pipe, into its thin place in the mold, steam piping into the night. Midnight waves lapped at the shore below them, lulling the metal into its new form.

"Well done," James said, drawing near once more. "But... there's one more."

One more? Had she missed something?

"Don't worry," James must have seen the alarm on her face. "That was perfect. But I have another mold for you to try. I thought—if you'll let me—we might pour this one together." He gestured to a boulder nearby, where a much smaller frame sat. She tipped her head to the side, pushed a flyaway curl out of her face as if the gesture could help her see beneath the surface of the sand filling the mold.

"What is it?"

James stirred the metal slowly. "It's... a promise. For someday."

"A pebble?" Aria brightened. Just like the old days. Except there was something different on his face. The glee of his youth, but matured. And...nervous.

"It is round, yes," he said. "And small. And a promise. But not a pebble."

Aria froze. The weight of his words shone in his eyes.

He lifted the ladle and opened his arm. She slipped in to his light embrace to slide her arm beneath his. Together they dipped into the crucible once more, and poured into the pipe of the smaller sand mold. The smell of sweet metal mixed with salt air tinged the night with warmth.

He slowly moved so that he was in front of her, the square wood-and-sand mold between them. "Someday," he said, "I will properly tell you, Aria St. John. How you are a song in a world of chaos." He folded her hands inside of his. "Someday I will properly ask you about what's in this box." He nodded at the mold. "Someday—that is, if you're of a mind to," his eyes crinkled at the sides and she heard the joy of a secret in his words. "We'll brush the sand away together and let this promise live." That calloused hand, in all its strength, rose to gently cup her face, twined it with the depth of all he was.

I will be of a mind to! She wanted to shout, sing it to the waves, holler it at the stars, whisper it straight to him. Instead, she stepped closer as he ran his hands up her arms to warm her. "James Shaw," she said, holding his name as she did his heart: like a treasure. "Pray tell, when is this 'Someday'?"

"That," he said, "I cannot tell you. But the question shall come. The promise will keep," he said. "Promises are for keeping, you know."

James leaned his forehead against hers, Aria leaned her head against his arm, twining her fingers with his. "Promises are for keeping," she said, and met his lips in a single, lingering kiss. A haven of memories and dreams to carry them into Christmas Eve.

- E P I L O G U E -

CHRISTMAS EVE SUMMONED the islanders together beneath its starry sky. Bundled in capes and blankets, they caroled soft tunes, jaunty tunes, holy tunes through town until all had joined up. The troupe wended their way through the tunnel, up the dune to the crest, where lanterns lined the path with dancing light.

Giovanni St. John took his sandy stage. The slightest tremor passed over him as he took a stately bow to his audience of villagers, farmers, and fishermen. Searching for someone, it seemed. There was a somber air of quiet hope about him. One that stayed with him through almost the whole performance.

Almost.

The time came for him to raise his hand for the

famous four-measure rest. The crowd sat in rapt silence, leaning forward with breath held to watch this man, whose power was still so palpable, simply stand. Head hung. No sign of his signature three-hundred-and-sixty-degree turn until, like a quiet tide rolling on delicate notes, the sound of a music box came.

Wordless, the familiar tune played, unfurling wonder in its familiar refrain:

Silent night,

Holy night,

All is calm,

All is bright...

Closer and closer it drew, as a woman all in wintry white spun a bicycle down that lantern-lit aisle on the dune. The audience released their breath, row by row until she passed by with her slow song of redemption.

Even after she stopped, the tune hung in the air. She stepped toward her father to whisper something in his ear. That brow of his furrowed, he stared at the moonlit bicycle that she gestured toward. Slowly, slowly, he reached through the silence. Grasped her hand and pulled her to the front of the orchestra with him. A question on her face, eyes bright, she looked up at him, and he gave a single nod. Together, they conducted through the swells and pulls of the finale.

It was this sight that met the Blacksmith as he crested the rise of the dune, shoulders rising and falling from his run. He'd lingered in the shadows long enough to see his Aria take flight on the bicycle, and stayed behind to hear the music play as the wheels he'd cast brought her closer to her father with every revolution.

And so it was that note by note, the Secret Symphony of Giovanni St. John whispered into the world with a thunder all her own: the Symphony that broke the silence of the night.

-THE END-

Twelve years ago, I sat in Trafalgar Square at St. Martin-in-the-Fields, candlelight flickering as the strains of a London orchestra filled the chamber. I'd gotten one of the "cheap seats"—you know, where there's a visual obstruction of some kind between you and the stage? But it didn't matter. I was transfixed.

At one point, the strings began this delicate interplay of notes, plucked with fingers, back and forth, dancing over the steady music beneath it. I remember smiling like a fool and leaning forward in my seat. My friend leaned in and whispered a word to me that I'll never forget: *pizzicato*. This plucking, this pizzicato, it positively ignited the music with life.

Looking at the journey of *Bespoke*, I see its own pizzicato. It was a story—just a string of word after word, moving through the rise and fall of plot structure. And then came the people. The friends, family, authors who came along, graciously alighted into the story, left their fingerprints and a bit of life until it became what it was.

Joanne Bischof and Kelli Standish. The wordsmith friends of my deepest heart, who listened to my ideas, read my words and offered encouragement, wisdom, and brilliance each in her own beautiful way. April, my beloved sister and friend, who so generously gave of her time and her musical knowledge and kept me from getting into too much treble (☺ Pun.). Jenni Brummet, who offered such helpful critiques. Jaime Wright, for so generously sharing with others about the *Bespoke* project.

Lesley Gore, and her beautifully encouraging heart and prayers at a moment's notice. Clarence thanks you!!

Laura Frantz, Lori Benton, Rachel McMillan, and Rel Mollet, who utterly astonished me with their generosity in (a) reading this tale, and (b) giving of their beautiful hearts, precious time, and treasured words to grace this book with their endorsements. I will never, ever be able to put into words what your kindness has meant, ladies! Perhaps I'll make you each a bicycle, instead.

Wendy Lawton, whose very voice instills peace and hope. Always the presence of encouragement and wisdom in her words.

Natalya Brown, for being an extraordinarily kind, intelligent help with the Gospel for Asia Bespoke project. Your passion and love of Christ are nothing short of inspiring, Natalya! And the Bespoke prayer team. You already know how grateful I am for you. You are the heartbeat of this little project, and I'm endlessly thankful.

To each reader who shared memories and ideas to be hinted at in this tale—I'm so grateful. Your stories are treasured.

My family—the boy with music and life in his laughter, and the girl with light and poetry in her words. You are my treasures! Ben. My Beloved. Who gave me a rock from the mountain we climbed the day he asked me for forever... thank you for being my living promise. Mom and Dad, incredible examples to me of a life rooted deep in love, steeped in wisdom, characterized by servant-hearted giving, and always encouraging on this writing journey. I love you!

Each of you, in your own cherished way, have ignited this piece with your own fingerprints, your own pizzicato.

Thank you.

Finally, and most importantly, a note about the heart where it all began: The Composer of our life songs, the Author of our stories, the Creator of light and warmth, the gentle Remover of our dross, Refiner of our hearts, Healer and Redeemer of our brokenness. When a story spills forth, my dearest desire is to find God's heartbeat in it. May the little words strung together in these pages speak of His Truth, His Love.

It's nice to think about, this idea of a bicycle bringing a melody. But while the fictional bicycle in *Bespoke* depended on bumps in a disc of metal for its tune, somewhere in the world a song so much richer plays.

It sings the words of life, brought by the hands of missionaries who bicycle into villages to minister to hungry hearts. In 2014, through God's faithfulness to do exceedingly, abundantly above all that we ask or imagine, something beautiful happened. The *Bespoke* project (www.mygfa.org/bespoke) was started with the hopes of funding just one bicycle for a Gospel for Asia national missionary-- but by the end of two months, through the mind-blowing generosity of readers, nearly *fifteen* bicycles were funded.

According to Gospel for Asia's website, "Many GFA-supported missionaries spend arduous hours walking from one village to another. With a bicycle a national missionary can visit three times as many villages in a day."

These missionaries bring such hope as they touch lives. Would you join me in praying for the hands that grip those very real bicycle handles? You can learn more about their ministry and specific prayer needs by visiting: http://www.gfa.org/pray/missionaries/

Amanda Dykes is a drinker of tea, a dweller of Truth, and a spinner of hope-filled tales, grateful for the grace of a God who loves extravagantly. A former English teacher, she has a soft spot for classic literature and happy endings.

Stop by for a virtual cup of tea and a visit at www.AmandaDykes.com, where she would love to connect with you!

-CARE TO CHIME IN?-

If you'd like to leave your thoughts on *Bespoke*, your review is most welcome at your favorite online bookshoppes and bookish gathering places, such a Goodreads.com. Thank you in advance for the gift of your musings and words!

MORE CHRISTMAS JOY...

Thank you for sharing your season with Aria and James! Before you go, it would be such a delight to offer you a gift.

***Tin Can Serenade,
a free short story,***
is available to download now at your preferred online bookseller.

Two homes in the mountains
Snowed in for winter's keep;
A river in between them,
A rope tight o'er the deep.
A mother and her daughter,
A father and his son,
A cottage and a cabin,
A story yet unspun
But time did freeze a tin can
Dangling from that rope
A messenger from days gone by,
Echoing long lost hope.
Until a cold November day
Saw decades fall away;
Young hands inscribed a folded scrap,
A missive sent to say...

So begins the plucky correspondence of Timothy and Genevieve, two children about to uncover a story long-buried... one filled with love, loss, and hope. An enchanting Christmas story laced with joy, God's healing hand in the broken places of life weaves through each letter passed over the river in that tin-can strung from the rusted pulley.

Enter into a simpler time in this petite tale, written to be just long enough to tuck into a stolen moment as you rest your feet and quiet your heart in the bustle of a busy season.

Made in the USA
Columbia, SC
25 March 2023

14260639R10067